The Day We Went to the Park

Original Origami Artwork by
Linda Stephen

Story by
Linda Stephen & Christine Manno

Handersen Publishing, LLC
Lincoln, Nebraska

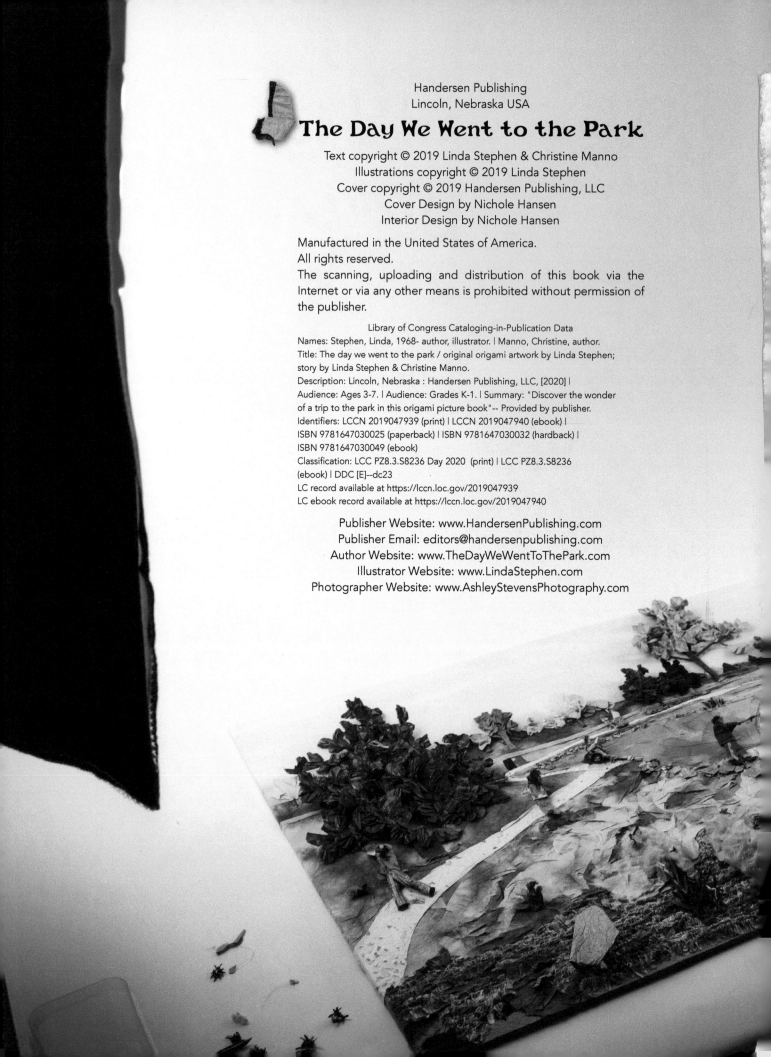

Handersen Publishing
Lincoln, Nebraska USA

The Day We Went to the Park

Library of Congress Cataloging-in-Publication Data
Names: Stephen, Linda, 1968- author, illustrator. | Manno, Christine, author.
Title: The day we went to the park / original origami artwork by Linda Stephen; story by Linda Stephen & Christine Manno.
Description: Lincoln, Nebraska : Handersen Publishing, LLC, [2020] |
Audience: Ages 3-7. | Audience: Grades K-1. | Summary: "Discover the wonder of a trip to the park in this origami picture book"-- Provided by publisher.
Identifiers: LCCN 2019047939 (print) | LCCN 2019047940 (ebook) |
ISBN 9781647030025 (paperback) | ISBN 9781647030032 (hardback) |
ISBN 9781647030049 (ebook)
Classification: LCC PZ8.3.S8236 Day 2020 (print) | LCC PZ8.3.S8236
(ebook) | DDC [E]--dc23
LC record available at https://lccn.loc.gov/2019047939
LC ebook record available at https://lccn.loc.gov/2019047940

Publisher Website: www.HandersenPublishing.com
Publisher Email: editors@handersenpublishing.com
Author Website: www.TheDayWeWentToThePark.com
Illustrator Website: www.LindaStephen.com
Photographer Website: www.AshleyStevensPhotography.com

For Solana, Sage and Sabine,
May you always find beauty in the world.
-L.S. and C.M.

Special thanks to photographers Ashley Stevens and Terri Huss and to early edits from Margo Foreman, Jane McGee. and Shelley Stoltenberg.

Inspired by Holmes Lake Park in Lincoln, Nebraska and Grand Lake Sailing in Presque Isle, Michigan.

The park by the lake is my favorite place to be.
So much to do! So much to see!

Come, and take a walk with me.

Scrunch, scrunch, scrunch.
Can you hear the gravel crunch?

Hi there, brown squirrel!
How are you this morn?

Have you found
a buried acorn?

Bushy-tailed squirrels scurrying to and fro.
Look at them jump! Look at them go!

If we crouch down low, what will we see?

A butterfly, four inchworms, and a honeybee.

Now, let's watch the inchworms scale that purple feathery flower.
Did you have any idea inchworms had that much power?

Do you think the butterfly and the busy honeybee
invited those inchworms home for some nectar and some tea?

We picked up a rock to look for slippery slugs...
and instead found a circle of...

lovely ladybugs

Let's count them all and watch them prance.
I did not know ladybugs knew how to dance.

High knees up! Two steps to the right.
Now, twirl all around and take a little flight.
Hey there, ladybugs, am I doing it alright?

Can you feel the gentle summer breeze?
Listen to the pine needles whispering in the trees.

I wonder what secrets they tell in the dark...
to the cardinal, the robin, and the western meadowlark?

There's so much to do here, and it's all for free!
Fly a kite, skip a rock, and even climb a tree!

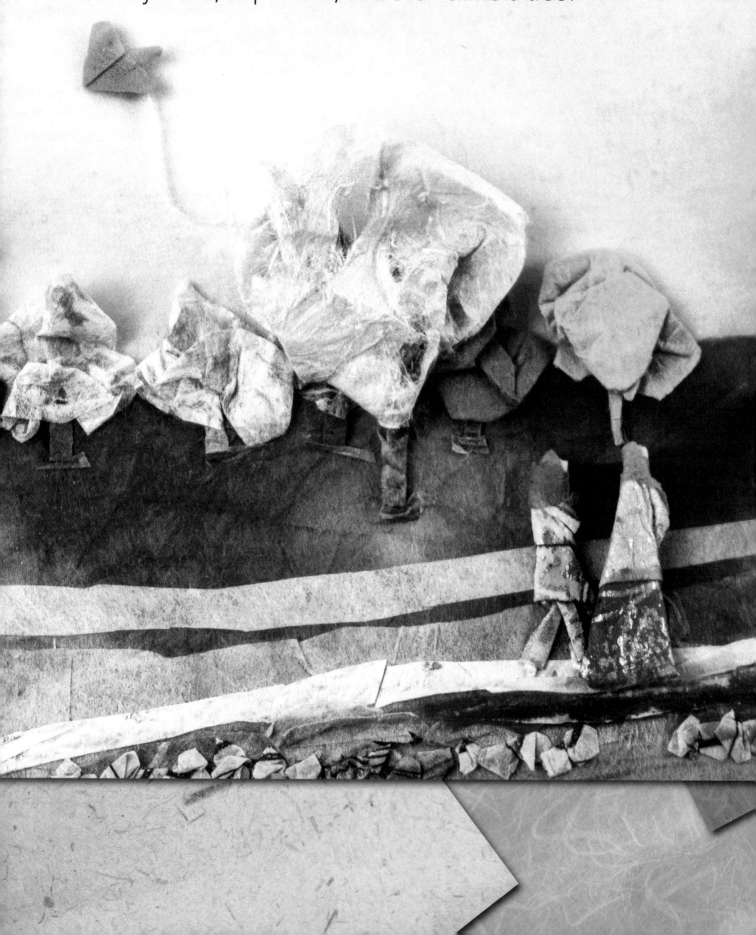

I can hop on one foot.
Hey! Look at me!

We could paint a picture
of the bobbing canoe,

catch two fish for dinner—
one for me, one for you.

We could dribble and play with our new soccer ball,
or watch a speedy spider scale a red-brick wall.

We could talk with a friend we've not seen in a while,
and wave to a baby who shares a great big smile.

We could lie on our backs and stare up at the trees.
I see a green scaly neck and dinosaur knees!

Or we could spy on that beetle skimming the top of the lake.
Think of the practice and the skill that must take.

We could try that! It sure looks like fun.

But we can't walk on water,
even if we run!

What a wonder to float in a boat on the water,
almost like that mother duck.

Oh, can you spot her?

Look out there in the middle of the lake!
It's a sail camp, and they're having a race!
Can you see the boat with the two sails that's setting the pace?

The wind's caught the sails. It's starting to blow.
The sailors pull their lines tight and off they go, go, go!

Jockeying for position, the sailors are learning to tack.
That means it's time to turn and make their way back.
Hey, be careful over there that the sheet is not slack!

As they come 'round the buoy,
they've reached the halfway mark.
Time to get to shore before it's completely dark.
I cannot believe they've sailed clear across the park.

Here come our friends.
I can see the grins on their faces.

It looks like they've had a great day at the races!

Rounding the bend after leaving the dock,
we meet a young person perched on a rock.

We poke in the shallows with a short, brown stick,
and see snails munching algae

while tadpoles learn

to flutter kick.

As we reach the end of our walk,
the cattails wave and sway.

The day we went to the park...

was perfect in every way!

Do it yourself!
Let's fold an origami caterpillar!

1. Start with a long rectangle of paper. Shown is 15 cm by 3.5 cm, 1/4 of a standard origami square.
2. Fold in half lengthwise.
3. Open again. Fold one corner to the center crease. Repeat 3 times.
4. There is a triangle tip at each end. On one end, fold the triangle in half. The tip should touch the base of the triangle.
5. At the other end, fold the entire triangle to the back. Open again. Turn over.
6. At the pointed end, fold up, then back 1/3 cm to make a pleat. Leave about 1.5 cm of tip free. Repeat the pleating pattern 6 to 10 times.
7. Flip over.
8. Fold left edge to center line.
9. Repeat on right side.
10. Fold in half.
11. Turn over. Hold both ends and gently pull out segments slightly to create a bending shape at the head, tail, or thorax.

Congratulations! You made a caterpillar. Try with other papers like office paper, gift wrap, or crepe paper.

Video and downloadable instructions at www.TheDayWeWentToThePark.com.

1

2

3a

3b

4

5

6a

6b

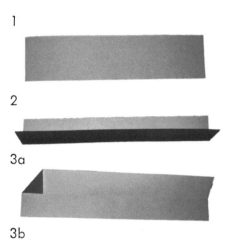

7

8

9

10

11

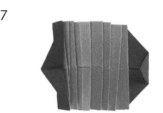

About the Authors

Linda Stephen is an award-winning paper artist whose artworks are part of public and private collections around the world. Her art is made entirely of paper: layers of Japanese handmade papers and her own invented origami sculptures. Linda grew up in Michigan playing outdoors in every season and later worked and studied in Japan for six years. She now lives in Lincoln, Nebraska with her family. She made her first origami model, a fortune teller, in fourth grade. www.LindaStephen.com.

Christine Manno is a university professor, world traveler, and knitter extraordinaire. In her free time, she enjoys long walks on crisp days with her French bulldog, Miss Daizy. Linda and Christine have been friends for over 30 years.

About the Art and Papers

Origami is the Japanese art of folding paper. In Japanese, "ori" means fold and "kami" means paper.

This art is made entirely of washi Japanese papers – plus some bookbinding glue. Japan has more handmade papers than the whole world combined. Artist Linda Stephen creates a watercolor look for the background through layering hand-dyed washi papers. Next, she invents 3D origami paper sculptures that add shadow, give dimension, and bring the work to life. This is an intricate process. The art for The Day We Went to the Park took more than 500 hours over six months and includes more than 300 papers in various patterns and textures and more than 1,000 paper sculptures.

CPSIA information can be obtained
at www.ICGtesting.com
Printed in the USA
BVHW020234030220
571171BV00003B/15